We Are Come to Die

a Drawn by the Frost Moon Novella

April W Gardner

ISBN: 978-1-945831-42-3
LCCN: 2023918011

Published by Big Spring Press
San Antonio, Texas
January 3, 2023

Printed in the United States of America.

April W Gardner's
Beneath the Blackberry Moon parts 1-3
(must be read in order)
Part 1: The Red Feather
Part 2: The Sacred Writings
Part 3: The Ebony Cloak
The Untold Stories (bonus material)

Drawn by the Frost Moon
(standalones)
Bitter Eyes No More
Love the War Woman
Finding Pretty Wolf
Strike of the Water Moccasin
We Are Come to Die

Visit aprilgardner.com and
subscribe to receive a free novel.

Message to Reader

Dear Reader,

We Are Come to Die is a novella that bridges my two series, Beneath the Blackberry Moon and Drawn by the Frost Moon. I wrote this story as a college assignment in the fall of 2022. Thanks, Prof. Cortez, for the incentive! My goal was to portray the final, decisive battle of the Creek War, Horseshoe Bend, and to give background on how True Seeker of *The Ebony Cloak* (aka Strong Bear of *Finding Pretty Wolf*) took on a vow to protect Polly Francis (aka Pretty Wolf). This is their full origin story.

It contains no spoilers unless read before book one of Beneath the Blackberry Moon. Chronological order places it before *The Ebony Cloak*. It overlaps with the first scenes of *Finding Pretty Wolf*, which is why it's part of the Drawn by the Frost Moon series.

My books typically have a Christ-centered theme, but because these characters meet the Savior in other books in the series, the only faith message I've been able to insert is a foreshadowing of their salvation. For that reason, I cannot label this book as Christian fiction but as clean historical fiction.

For a fuller reader experience, you'll find a glossary at the end for the words underlined throughout.

Enjoy!

April W Gardner
aprilgardner.com

Table of Contents

THE HORSE'S FLAT Foot was nothing as I'd imagined. Under the stars of our three-day journey to the battle site, I'd lain awake long into the nights and worked to picture the rumored field and wall. In my mind, it had amounted to a flat, empty stretch of grass the span of my old township's stickball grounds. A pine-pole picket sectioned off the broadest side. Campfires dotted the space, and warriors, painted in the colors of war, spent their days in practice, shooting arrows into the hearts of Bluecoat effigies made of straw. During their preparations to meet Old Sharp Knife Jackson's army, they laughed, they cheered, they teased.

Quite a vision, by my reckoning. A vision that reality swiftly turned a sickly pale gray.

Reality was an undulating meadow so large I could hold out my thumb toward the forest's edge on the far side and block out the women carrying baskets.

Reality was a collection of small timber barricades all angled toward the main, snaking structure, a barricade that unhinged my jaw.

Reality was no mere wall but a log-and-earth bulwark so thick I could rest my head on one side, stretch myself out reaching with my big toe, and touch only air.

Reality was an army of men a thousand strong. Bedraggled and unpainted, they went about organizing ammunition, repairing and cleaning weapons, laying the final logs on their months-long project. Not a laugh, cheer, or tease among them.

Old to young, lines scored their faces, their brows heavy with thought. Perhaps with the burden of preserving the Old Path, that of the <u>Muscogees</u>, my people. The fire of battle blazed in every eye. Just the same, death lived in their aspects. It lived in the deepest grooves bracketing their mouths and in the way they looked tenderly upon the serving women. As if memorizing the softness of their features and the scale of their vulnerability, as if storing away the details to pull them out later and use to reload their resolve.

At the sight of the warriors' morose disposition, malaise struck my belly. It cramped inside me. Having lived through the <u>Confederacy's</u> civil strife and the ensuing Red Stick War with the Bluecoats, I was no stranger to the horrors of battle. I had taken no lives, but I'd seen plenty taken, including those of my mother, her mother, and every clan member between. Only her brother remained. He walked beside me now.

Keeps Watch Hardjo, my *pawa* and clan elder, kept pace on my left. The heft of his muscled hand warmed the back of my neck and guided me through the bustling activity. Despite his hand's reassuring squeeze, sweat broke out on my palms. I clutched the satchel hooked over my shoulder and swallowed the bile burning the back of my throat.

As I glanced about me and took in the grief peering at me from a thousand dark eyes, I came to understand a matter. About our mission. About courage. For we had not come to this place to earn feathers or titles or battle honors we might boast about in our gray years.

We had come to the Horse's Flat Foot to die.

~ ~ ~

I knew the battlefield's center of command by the cluster of heavily feathered warriors and by the profusion of scars decorating their flesh. Seated on logs, they congregated about a low-burning fire. A battered and blackened copper kettle sat on the exterior coals. Though it rattled and steamed with enthusiasm, none turned its way. Their heads were put together, their volume high and strung tight with the strain of encroaching battle.

My pawa and I stopped some ten strides out, far enough from the _miccos_ to not be accused of lending ears to their designs. A daytime moon, round and dim, hung several handbreadths above their heads. Flawless in its span of blue, the sky would soon relinquish Grandfather Sun. As he sank behind the pines at my back, Grandmother would shine down on the miccos in fullest brilliance. A blessing? A showering of strength? Every soul present could use both in basket loads.

I canted in to speak low. "Which is the micco?"

There could be several of varied ranks among the group, for this final battlefield was a meeting place of survivors from across our once-great Confederacy. But my pawa—and perhaps any other present—would know which micco I meant, the one spoken of reverently in the river's presence lest <u>Water Spirit</u> take affront.

Pawa Keeps Watch tipped his head to mine and directed his sight to the left of the gathering. "The one there with the armed guard standing behind."

I stared at the only one he could mean. No other had a man at his back. "Blue shirt and turban?"

"Mm."

"He is not what I imagined."

The indigo dots tattooed across my pawa's forehead rounded into an arch. "And how had you imagined?"

Dared I say it? I passed a dampening tongue over my lips. "Towering. Muscular." I grinned and added, "Fangs and talons."

In short, formidable. The opposite of the fellow squatting on a log, knees splayed, ankles crossed. One arm folded over his flat belly, he tugged at his lower lip while listening to the animated chatter swirling about him.

A chuckle rumbled out of Pawa Keeps Watch. "The spirits use whom they will, Nephew. And who are you to judge by appearance, eh?" On an ironic torque of the lips, he pinched the skin at the back of my arm hard enough to leave a long memory.

As taught, I took the rebuke in silence. It was my due, after all, and better from Pawa Keeps Watch than the spirits.

While we waited to be noticed, I cast about to learn the area. The barricade zigzagged to our right some fifty paces distant, and to our immediate left sat another grouping of men. This one was smaller yet far more intriguing, not for the ten-musket stand presiding over the setting or for the portable table, but for the man bent over the map stretched across its surface.

Though he wore the long-shirt, breechcloth, and leggings of a Muscogee male, the skin covering the nicked hands splayed flat on the map was as white as mother's milk. For long, impolite moments, I gaped at the top of his head of closely cropped brown hair, until I found my senses and elbowed my pawa's side. "Look there, Pawa. A white man stands with us."

The man in question flicked his gaze up at me, and I startled on the spot. Thick black lashes rimmed eyes the pale blue of a winter sky. His mouth spread in a grin before he blinked one eye as if in a spasm. My frown of confusion only broadened his smile.

"You embarrass yourself," my pawa said on a brusque hush. "Blabbing as if the man cannot understand you. Behaving as if you've never seen a white man in your life."

"I haven't," I countered at matched volume, even as heat climbed my throat for having been so narrow of mind. "Anyway, not one who carries the Red Stick war club." Granted, he also wore a sacred medicine bundle.

If he sought protection of the spirits, same as the rest, perhaps he was not so foreign as his skin accused.

"I admit they are a rarity, but do not be caught speaking ill of this one. He is—"

"Oi!"

My pawa's head swiveled up and around. "Ah, we are noticed at last."

I followed his gaze to the miccos and the mid-aged fellow who had clued into our presence. He sat upright, surprise bright on his features. Donning a grin, he lifted his arm high. When my pawa returned the gesture, the man pushed to standing and jogged our way. The rest showed no more than a flick of curiosity at the man's departure before returning to their discussion.

As he closed the distance, the tassels trailing the outsides of his patched leggings bounced with the irregular pattern of his gait. Did he bear some invisible wound? If so, the delight crinkling his eyes gave no indication of pain.

"Keeps Watch," he called ahead of himself, "you dog, where have you been hiding yourself?"

"As far from your earth-rumbling snores as I could get." My pawa outstretched his arm. "Nokose, my old friend. We are come."

"You are come, indeed." Nokose clasped him at the forearm and brought him firmly against his chest to join their hearts. "At long last, too." He pushed them apart and gave my uncle's cheek a set of slaps that had the sound of smarting. "I'd thought to have escaped ever spying this ugly face again."

Pawa Keeps Watch belted a laugh. "Pity on you then, for you must spy it this once more."

He wouldn't be heard denying the accusation. Of the twins, Keeps Watch's sister had received all the beauty, while he'd received all the charm. As for myself, I liked to think I'd acquired a fair mix of both, for charm could be learned, and my pawa was a faithful teacher.

"Have you come to swap insults with me," Nokose said, "or should I take you before the micco as new volunteers, you and—" Shifting to me, he landed a brisk palm on my own cheek, confirming the sting theory. "Who is this?"

I resisted the urge to rub it out and returned him the smile, albeit a statelier version. My face was youthful enough without adding a cheeky grin to it. "I am True Seeker."

"Save your timidity for the Bluecoat musket balls, boy. Tell me something of yourself. Do you stick to Rabbit?" He indicated my bare chest and the rabbit tattoo pricked into my flesh.

"I do. Same as my Pawa Keeps Watch. My mother was Tall Woman of Alabama Town." My throat threatened to close around her name, but I dashed away the grief and, for good measure, added a degree of lift to my chin.

"Tall Woman, eh?" Head cocked and mouth turned down, Nokose swept his sight down the length of me. "How many winters have you seen?"

Smothering my aggravation—was his questioning not valid?—I stretched my spine to its greatest height, which admittedly was not great at all. I couldn't help my hunger-shriveled state.

"Fourteen." I inhaled deep to expand my ribs and held the haul as Nokose arched an eyebrow and studied me through narrowed, thinking eyes.

The look sent my heartbeats tripping. My pawa had lauded this man as a talented battle strategist. Perhaps, he pondered where best to use me on the battlefield. Or whether to use me at all.

At last, he said, "So tell me, True Seeker of Rabbit, what skills do you have to recommend you?"

A question with a sticky answer. "My arrows fly true. I can drive one through a chicken from twenty paces."

"Ah, but does your bow work on Bluecoats as well as on chickens?"

It had been too much to hope a chief, even a lesser one, would not see through my thin tolerance for war and my underdeveloped courage. My shoulders lowered a degree. "I have yet to take a life."

"Four full seasons of war and no opportunity has presented to defend yourself?"

My pawa replaced his palm on my neck and nudged me closer to his side, a claiming gesture that smoothed the cadence of my pulse. "I am my nephew's defense until he is grown. Or until the day arrives I am no longer able."

"As you should be, my friend." Nokose's chin descended in concession. "You are a fortune boy indeed to have such an able defender. In such desperate times, we rely on each other and…" Eyes going distant, he tinkered with an amulet strung to his wrist by a leather thong. "And on Creator."

"True, true." After a glance to me, my pawa cleared his throat. "Our township is finished, Nokose. We are all who remain of Rabbit of Alabama Town. Do take me to the micco. I shall tell him True Seeker and I come to add our bows to the effort. As for where to station my nephew, he makes a reliable ammunition mule, and you will not find a male with more heart for guarding the helpless."

As he spoke, I maintained unwavering contact with Nokose's penetrating gaze. "My pawa knows me well. Use me as you wish, war chief."

If Nokose sent me to Tohopeka, the village they'd built in the woods for the women and children, I would not slump in shame. I would streak my face black with ash. I would arrange the arrows in my quiver for quickest grab, and I would go down bleeding before any enemy who dared approach the innocents.

Though I had been exposed to violence aplenty, I had not much cared for it, not where it involved men and death. The defense of innocents was another matter, one I took to with relish.

Nokose's eyes twinkled. "So I will."

While he and my pawa finished their pleasantries, my attention snagged on a female gliding through the warriors and coming, it would appear, toward...me? *Pray spirits, yes.* For though her confident bearing and unusual height declared her my senior by as much as five winters, I would not shun an opportunity to know such a woman.

Both her trim build, that of a woman not yet a mother, and the long black hair rippling loose about her, suggested maiden status. Regardless, I wouldn't wager even the unfinished arrow in my quiver that she was available, for in addition to all that, she possessed a comely air.

Even from where I stood a little distance off, I could appreciate her elegant features: the high cheekbones and thick upper lids that bespoke her Muscogee blood; the straight, narrow nose and lighter skin that suggested a mingling of white heritage. Unless she opened her mouth and revealed a set of snaggled teeth, she was quite possibly the loveliest creature I'd ever encountered.

All this being the case, was it any wonder she caught every male eye on her passage through the camp? Or that mine had stuck to her like two beetles upended in sap?

Several stood as she passed, greeting her with soft words and dipped chins as if, oddly enough, she were a clan mother, elder, or even a micco. Wearing an open smile to stun the heart—not a snaggle to be seen—she returned every greeting and dispensed a few of her own, unsolicited but lapped up like _sofki_ on a hot summer day. Indeed, what man would not want that beauty directed at him, however platonic?

If any existed, I was not among them.

"True Seeker."

My shoulders jounced, the call of my name unpeeling me from the woman. Blinking, I found my pawa alone. Nokose had returned to the council, presumably, to request an audience for us before Micco Crazy Medicine. "Yes, Pawa?"

The wag of his fingers urged me closer. "If the micco requests us both," he murmured, "say nothing unless addressed. Micco Crazy Medicine is unpredictable and has strong magic. I would not wish you to come down on his foul side for any reason."

"As you say, Pawa." I, too, did not wish to fall on the micco's less-pleasant side. Stories circulated of how Water Spirit had once blinded him with a vision, then restored his sight and commanded him to purge white ways from their borders. Such power was beyond my comprehension. I was content to stay my distance.

"You are a fine boy, True Seeker." As he looked down on me, the brown of his eyes glistened with unshed tears. "My sister would be proud. As am I. I will be prouder yet when you survive this place and find some pretty girl or two and convince them you will make a proper mate. Settle down in Alabama Town. Rebuild. What do you say?" He sniffed and blinked away excess moisture, his eyes now twinkling another way. "Can you manage it?"

No man was as efficient at sending heat to my cheeks as Keeps Watch, as he did now. Partially because his exploits were many, as would be his expectations. Partially because I could not keep my gaze from darting to the sole woman among us—there and back to my pawa.

Long enough to note she now stood beside the sole white man among us. That flick of a glance had caught her leaned over the table with him, fist pressed to mouth as if in contemplation. The confusion of that image, the improbability of it—of a young woman strategizing with a white man over a Red Stick battlefield—almost shackled my thoughts. It certainly stuttered my tongue. "Would it not be, that is, I should find other Rabbit and settle where they are." For lineage passed through the mother. No number of wives would change that. If I wanted to rebuild Rabbit Clan, I could not do that through marriage.

"Once you are established, other members of Rabbit will join you. Someone must be the first to resettle Alabama Town, yes? And how better to rebuild than with a wife at your side?"

Knowing my role, I nodded along. The newcomers would have children to nurture and love, boys to instruct in the ways of the People. A man lived with his wife's clan but raised his sister's children rather than his own. While I had no sister, I could be adopted as brother. Clan was clan, after all, no matter the distance. And after the war, there would be a tremendous want of men.

"I wish you to settle down at the old site, True Seeker, and make it new again. It was your mother's dream, you know, and it is mine. Can you make it yours?"

The weighty question bent my head. As I let it lumber through my thoughts, I toed channels into the dirt. Could I find a wife? Naturally. I might not have the full charm of Keeps Watch of Alabama Town, but I'd always held my own where the females were concerned.

Could I somehow rebuild an abandoned, possibly destroyed, village and convince distant clan to join me in making it lively and beautiful again? Alone? Without my pawa? Here, my confidence waned.

There was a reason Nokose Fixico had looked upon my fledgling frame with half-concealed chagrin. Lodges did not construct themselves. Corn fields did not plant themselves. Rabbits did not snare themselves. Borders did not guard themselves.

And yet, the dream held such sweetness I could taste it on my tongue. Contrasted with it was the bitterness of how my pawa spoke as if he would not be there to assist. As if his blood were already soaking into the soil beneath our feet.

I lifted my head and faced him squarely. "We will do it together." Denial wrinkled the fleshy spot between Pawa Keeps Watch's eyes, but I would not hear it. I would not allow him to voice his death into being. "There might be a pretty girl out there for you, too," I tacked on, aiming for distraction. "You are not *so* old."

Certain lines around his eyes gave way to others, these more acceptable to my raucous nerves. "Not old at all, you nipping pup." Broadcasting threat through bared teeth, he glanced a mock blow off the back of my head, then snorted humor from his nose. "But no, I have already had my pretty girls. I pass that honor to you. And I imagine it is with great honor and delight that you receive it."

We shared an eye-scrunching grin, but I made no reply. What need was there to confirm it? Any who lived beyond this battle would be doing so to their fullest. Pursuing peace, dreams, and yes, love...

"You have a good eye for women, Nephew. But not that one."

The warning timbre of my pawa's voice jerked my attention off the woman. Until that instant, I hadn't realized my attention had migrated back. It bounced off her and, by default, onto the next nearest subject— blue eyes that pierced me through. I jerked again and whipped my head back to safer lands—my pawa's stern expression.

"What, Pawa?"

My feigned ignorance found no traction, for Keeps Watch gave his head a single brisk shake. "Any woman but that one, True Seeker. If she is who I think, she is betrothed to that gem-eyed Englishman."

"Who is he?"

"Among his people, he is of noble blood. As recently as last winter, he fought in the ranks of their Redcoats, raising arms against our shared, blue-coated foe. After the war, he wishes to establish a trade store to keep us stocked in arms and munitions. But now, here, among us, he is a warrior who sympathizes with our cause. For his bravery at the Battle of Emuckfaw and for his fierce loyalty to the Defiance, he is called Iron Wood."

My eyebrows climbed. The white man had been granted a warrior's name? The fact drew me back to the couple. Mouth moving, voice a low hum, the woman rapped the map with a commanding finger. When Iron Wood nodded, she smiled adoringly, then brushed her lips across his and took her leave.

Something slithered through my middle, and I didn't like to name it. Blue eyes met mine again, inquiring in aspect. I turned away, murmuring, "Then he is important, indeed."

"Important enough to make critical ties through marriage. Iron Wood has earned his betrothal."

"And the English do not share." The new voice brought our focus around to Nokose who limped to rejoin us. He wore a skewed grin that rankled my pride and nudged a nonchalant shrug out of me.

"She is not wed *yet*," I said as casual as you please, not a care that this Iron Wood fellow could hear or understand. "In time, I could convince her and her clan mother I am the stronger match."

The elder males laughed in tandem as if they'd practiced. "Ah," Nokose drew out, "but could you convince her micco father?" He turned his head in a deliberate arc, directing my focus to the lone figure remaining at the fire.

"She is the daughter of Micco Crazy Medicine?" My voice pitched high, cracking on the way up.

To my shame, the sound exploded another bout of laughter from the men. My pawa went so far as to ruffle the hair on my heat-prickled scalp. "I see you are beginning to understand now, Nephew."

Heat scorched my neck, but bless the spirits, Nokose took pity on me and popped my pawa on the arm. "Leave him be, Keeps Watch. Come. The micco will see you now."

"*Maddo*," my pawa said, thanking him. Rumbling with low laughter, he began that way.

Shoulders stooped, I made to follow, but Nokose blocked me with the bar of his lifted arm.

"Not you, my bold, young friend." He turned to follow my pawa, saying over his shoulder as he went,

"Perhaps, take the opportunity to begin your conquest."

Chapter 2

"DO NOT MIND Nokose. He picks at those he likes." Iron Wood lifted his voice but left his attention on the crude map spread under his hands. None would mistake who'd spoken. He was aware the slurry of his English tongue forming the <u>Muskogee</u> language was signal enough.

Besides, Iron Wood was yet unwilling to release the hope that, if he stared long enough, he might use his many years as a marine in His Majesty's Royal Navy to find a path forward. One that included a positive outcome for the <u>Red Sticks</u>. Victory at best. At worst, survival.

The last, he knew, was a fool's prayer. These warriors were set on their path. They would streak toward their enemy and own this field, or they would make their war cries serve as death rattles. The American army marching toward them was days off, but already, grief sat like a stone in Iron Wood's stomach, heavy and cold. Unmovable. As unalterable as the Red Sticks' course. But they could do no other.

As a former officer in the British marines, Iron Wood had unique insight into General Andrew Jackson's ambitions regarding this land, a thing that had once meant little to him. Before Polly, the Red Stick movement had been an inconsequential detail delaying his dreams of owning a lucrative trading establishment. With Polly, he could not unsee the imminent destruction of a beautiful way of life, could not blow from his nose the stench of ash wafting off a once-proud nation. When she had become his own, promising to wed him upon war's completion, so had her people and her cause.

He saw it now, the blight that General Jackson was on Muscogee lands, on humanity itself. The general must be stopped, and this undulating expanse of grass was as good a spot as any to see it done.

Iron Wood smoothed a palm over the wrinkled map, passing scuffed finger pads over the inlet at the river's sharpest bend. This exercise in cartography hadn't been completely pointless. He'd established a fallback point for Polly and a means of escape. If she would take it. Moments ago, she hadn't seemed particularly willing to hear him out, merely rapping out defensive locations around Tohopeka he must strengthen.

Clever, aggravating woman. Did she not realize she was the future of this band? She *must* survive. But no. She would rather play the war chief and turn his hairs gray along with her father's. How very fortunate for her they both loved her so dearly.

"Does he pick at your white skin?" The boy's question, spoken with a thick lining of suspicion, jolted Iron Wood out of his grim musings.

Earlier, he'd studied the boy thoroughly enough, heard him clearly enough to know the fabric of him and to confidently make his choice. Even so, he raised his eyes now for a closer inspection. Two tattered braids hung over his collarbones, bare of feathers, beads, or bands. Since he was attired in only skin and breechcloth, a solid indigo rabbit tattoo was visible where it leaped across his left breast.

His boyish frame was on full gangly display. Elbows, knees, ears, hip bones: he was all knobs and protrusions, and everywhere on him were angles. Where his neck met his shoulder. Where his ribs banked down along his sides. Where his cheekbones slanted high.

His jaw, though, hewn broad and sharp, was more man than boy. A strange contrast to his reed-thin neck. Every Red Stick on Horse's Flat Foot, especially their children, wore the face of hunger, but what had this one's mother been feeding him? Water and air?

Didn't matter, for the valiant heart in his chest outweighed the rest of him altogether, and for the task Iron Wood had in mind, heart was what mattered most. It helped that the boy had gazed on Iron Wood's betrothed as if she'd set the stars a-twinkle in the sky. That he now brazenly questioned a white man's presence on this battlefield only solidified Iron Wood's decision.

The boy would do.

Iron Wood couldn't help the smile tugging at the corner of his lips. "Your name is True Seeker, so tell me. What truths do you seek?"

Saying nothing, the boy's judging eyes fell to Iron Wood's medicine bundle where it dangled over the table. Iron Wood pushed upright and tucked the pouch under his shirt, placing it close to his heart.

At last, eyes narrowed, True Seeker spoke his demand. "Why are you here?"

Iron Wood thought about giving the lighter of the two reasons he stood on this field, but as deeply as he loved Polly, he sensed True Seeker wanted something yet deeper. He loosened the strings of the accessories pouch tied to his belt and pulled out a much-abused newspaper clipping, one passed around during his days in His Majesty's Royal Navy, back when he'd been Lord Robert Maxwell Bellamy, a major in the Blue Marines. He and his fellow officers had studied the image as well as the man, so they might know against whom they hurled their cannonballs.

Unfolding it, Iron Wood pressed it flat to the wobbly table and slid it toward the boy.

True Seeker brought it near his nose for close inspection, then held it out, angling it this way and that, setting the general's white hair aflame with the orange rays of the dying sun. Finally, he asked, "Whose image is this?"

"A white chief of the Americans. He is known for using the People to advance his rank. He strives to be chief of all Americans from the Great Waters to here, Muscogee territory, and beyond."

"Head chief?" A wrinkle formed on True Seeker's nose. "Do you mean to say he wishes to be the White Father in Washington?"

The boy had a better grasp of American politics than Iron Wood had given him credit for. "So he says. So his actions say." He nudged up one shoulder, making light of his conjectures, but in his heart, in the finest creases of his soul, he believed it gospel. "If the general clears this land of obstacles to settlers, he will be praised for it, you see. The Americans will choose him above others to lead their country. Then he will move on to remove other nations native to this territory so he might merge the land with those they already own. Any who stands in his path will be sliced down."

Iron Wood paused to allow the knot in his throat to subside. The tepid March breeze sifted through his long-shirt and cooled his heated skin. Such pestilent thoughts never failed to spring sweat from his pores. "If we allow it to go on, True Seeker, there will not remain a man of your skin for a thousand <u>sights</u>."

But not Iron Wood's Polly. No, his would never allow it.

She refused to leave her father's side, and Iron Wood refused to leave hers. So here they were, and here he stood, staring at a map and praying to his mother's Jesus and to his betrothed's spirits and to the woman herself that she might be preserved. He only wished to spare her further exposure to death. But, gads, she made it difficult.

"Are you a prophet?"

The sincere inquiry sprang a smile to Iron Wood's lips. "I am only a former soldier who understands the desires and the methods of the white chiefs."

"Then it is good we have you, Iron Wood." Nodding, True Seeker screwed up his mouth as if he'd bitten into an unripe scuppernong. Pinching the paper between two fingers, he dropped the clipping, face-up, onto the tabletop. "This is Old Sharp Knife," he stated.

Ah, that explained the sour expression, as well as the straying of Iron Wood's fingers to the knife sheathed at his thigh. "General Andrew Jackson. The very same." The blade slipped free. He pointed its tip toward the sun where it sank into the structure they'd spent the last two months building. "The same who, in two days, will send his Bluecoats against that wall."

Disdainful air jetted through True Seeker's nose. "They will die in the attempt."

"Many will, yes."

"The prophets assure us they will not get through." His voice rose, words overly firm as if to convince himself rather than Iron Wood.

Sympathizing with the urge, Iron Wood indulged in a moment of admiration for the barricade's expert engineering: parallel rows of logs stacked six high to create mirror walls, packed soil between the walls, two ranges of loopholes angled in such a way the enemy would subject themselves to crossfire should they attempt to scale. A stunning feat of architecture, indeed. Doubtful even a 6-pounder could rattle the structure.

If only an unyielding barricade were enough.

Iron Wood's next indulgence came in the form of a reassuring smile for the boy. "The prophets are likely correct." His demeanor must have lacked a certain something, for the boy's brows tugged together.

"But?" Brow furrowed. True Seeker gazed down on the map as if Iron Wood had read a warning scrawled in the map's legend.

Iron Wood knew from experience no solutions would be found there or anywhere on that map, on that field. Not keen to destroy the boy's hopes, he said nothing. Only let him study the land's contours and ponder their predicament.

The boy traced a finger along the map's key features, then paused on the stick figures representing each army. One red. Five blue.

"They will not come through our wall." When True Seeker's eyes lifted off the map, they shone dark with unrepressed fear. "But they will come over it," he finished on a hoarse whisper.

"Perhaps." Perhaps not. There was a chance they would weary of slaying red men and go home to their wives. There was also a chance God would send the Angel of Death to slaughter them as they slept. Iron Wood wouldn't count on either.

"And if they do?" True Seeker pressed. "If Old Sharp Knife comes over our wall?"

"If they do, if Jackson crosses that line,"—Iron Wood stretched his lips into a wicked grin and, using the tip of his blade, pinned the general through the eye—"I will drop him where he stands."

~ ~ ~

At the Tallapoosa's slippery brink, Polly glanced back like a child making sure her parent hadn't caught her being naughty. In this case, it was Iron Wood's notice she wished to avoid. But she'd made him no promises to go straightaway to Tohopeka, and she *did* plan to shelter there. Eventually.

Satisfied she'd arrived unseen, she made her way to the riverbank, noting the man-sized footprints pressed into the sand. They led from her father's discarded moccasins into the water and told her he communed with that spirit now. Although, how he could, she did not know. The water slapped almost violently against the bank, stretching its confines and daring any would-be invader to try its strength. Even with the Bluecoats bearing down, she felt safe.

She chose a patch of dirt on which to settle herself and, dividing her unkempt tresses into three sections, began braiding. Her fingers were threading sleepily through the familiar motions when the water broke over her father's head. A proud smile eased across her as she worked a leather thong around the braid's tail and watched the legend emerge from his prayers with Water Spirit.

Her father, Crazy Medicine, rose steady and straight like an oak trunk breaking ground in a spirit world where natural laws held no sway. Eyes closed, arms held out at his sides, he splayed his fingers over the choppy surface and let the river dance about him, through him, down him.

He angled his face to the morning sun, the expansive inflating of his ribs the only indication he'd been deprived of air longer than any ordinary human should. But throughout the Confederacy, no one disputed that Crazy Medicine—micco, prophet, rebel— was anything but ordinary.

Water Spirit *spoke* to him. Oh, for such a gift!

Polly well remembered cranking her neck back to gaze up at him from her niggling six-winters' height and dreaming of the day some spirit might deem *her* worthy to receive a vision powerful enough to blind her. For a period of ten <u>sleeps</u>, she'd led her father about by the hand. The day he recovered his sight, he began preaching of founding a strictly Red Stick town, and from that dream, Holy Ground was born.

"Holy Ground," she muttered, stroking her silver-set moonstone ring. "Village of blood and ash." Realizing she was trapped again between Bluecoats and a river, Polly loosed a cynical laugh.

The noise brought her father's lashes up from his prayers. At the sight of her, they flared wide, then he grinned and pushed toward shore, his breechcloth dragging behind. "Why I continue to be surprised that my little *miccohokti* is always exactly where she needs be, I do not know." He hauled himself onto the grass so that he stood over her, water spitting onto her upturned face.

"Tell that to Iron Wood." She swiped droplets from the bridge of her nose. "And hear how he contradicts you."

"He would never." Her father began wringing the river from his silver-threaded hair. "Does the rabbit taunt the wolf? Iron Wood never forgets I am micco, and he is white."

Polly blinked at him. Iron Wood was no defenseless rabbit. And what had the color of his skin to do with anything? Both her parents were half-bloods. Polly herself could pass for a sun-browned settler or a Spaniard. She twisted at the waist, fronting her father with pinned-back shoulders. "He is also the ship that will sail you to his King George."

Ire flashed hot across the micco's face.

Swift as her next breath, Polly shielded herself with lowered lashes. "Forgive me. I misspoke."

"So you did." On a stout exhale, Crazy Medicine plucked up his deerskin hunting shirt. "But...he is your chosen, and duty demands you defend him." He shoved his arms into the garment, then reached for his leggings, looking up while bent double to cut her a look. "Even against Water Spirit's prophet and your micco." A backhanded acceptance of apology, but she would take it, for an apology from Crazy Medicine came along as often as a three-legged cock.

"Maddo, Father."

While he strapped on his bandoleer, then his weapon's belt, then his moccasins and sash, his thoughts seemed pulled elsewhere.

She fidgeted with the shredded ends of the dingy purple ribbon that laced her blouse. "Where do your thoughts take you, Father?"

He stilled, his feathered turban cocked midway to its seat on his head. "To what I've been shown." His line of sight stretched out before him, seemingly to the willow leaned precariously over the opposite shore. She knew the look and became stone-still. A few bats of his lashes, then he spoke, soft and deliberate. "For us here behind the wall, it is victory or death. There is no between. No compromise."

"None, Father." Did he fear her resolve had somehow been shaken, jeopardized? "No concession is worth so much as the ink in Old Sharp Knife's treaty quill." She spouted his own words back at him, which brought his eyes her way. They were a set of lances, thrilling her blood with their battle-ready edge.

"Old, mad Jackson has written my death song. He vows to sing it himself while burning our villages like sacred fires to his white god. Farmers, cattlemen, trappers, they come at his urging and will not be content until they own every hill, doe, and corn plant in Muscogee country." The same anger-goading, blood-rushing story the warriors rehearsed before every engagement.

His passion drove her to her feet.

"But I make my own vow, Daughter, and it is this: I will not see <u>Grandmother Sun</u> rise on the day these terrible things come to pass." His voice rose by degrees, his body vibrating with a decade of fury. "I say that after eleven bloody moons of battle and flight, it is here we will stand. There is no surrender, no retreat. Whether on this ground or in the Florida Point for those who've not joined us today, we will stand, war clubs raised, until there is none left to do so!"

On that fiery exclamation, he descended to his haunches. The fringe of his yellow sash mingled with the tall grasses as his long fingers wrapped about the hilt of the silver dagger resting on the ground beside his hatchet. Soundlessly, he slid the work of art from its sheath, his breaths steadying. Sunlight caught in its glassy polish and ran to the tip of its silver, hand-length blade. He turned the weapon this way and that, examining every nook and curve of its antler handle.

Solemnly, he stood, took her hand in his, and laid the dagger in her palm. "You are to have this."

Jaw hung, she stared at him. "But it's your—"

"I know what it is." He curled her fingers about the stiff leather casing and presented her a wry smile. "Seeing I crafted it myself." He'd done so after receiving the rank of big warrior.

An accomplished silversmith, Crazy Medicine celebrated victory somewhat differently than most. A broach for her sister upon her first visit to the women's moon lodge. A tobacco box for himself when he returned from a campaign with Major Beasley's hair in his fist. A pair of teardrop earbobs for her mother when she became clan mother.

Polly spun her ring, her last trinket from that peaceful season, and the only piece he'd allowed her to keep. From a ring to...what? Giving her the symbol of his leadership and cunning in battle? "Why? Why *this*? Why me?"

"When the time comes, little miccohokti, you will know." The words traveled on a pained whisper, as if having bloodied themselves on the way out, and Polly's stomach coiled with dread.

She tiptoed into her next question. "What exactly did Water Spirit show you?"

His lips bowed earthward, warbling the rows of horizontal lines inked into the skin beneath his eyes. "The People's adversary, a bleeding heart, and you."

Her brain seized. Her field of vision narrowed to the blade in her possession.

The adversary's head...by her hand?

"M-me?" At the weak sound of her own voice, shame heated her cheeks. Surely, Water Spirit expected better of her than shrinking like a lost little girl.

Eyes grave, her father dipped a lone nod, and the knots in her middle screwed so tight they stirred up acid. The knife reclined between her open hands, looking so innocent and beautiful. On its surface, a strip of her face reflected her glossy lower lip hanging separately from its trembling partner.

Polly was a born fighter, but her usual weapons consisted of debate, savvy, even humor. Knives? Bleeding hearts?

Spirits shield her, but she didn't want this. Not the dagger, not the rare insecurity shading her father's countenance, and indeed not the prophecy.

Fingers shaking, she secured the sheathed blade to her waist sash. "Anything else you wish to tell me, Father?"

Leaking a long breath, he aligned a flat hand with the side of her face and crooked a sad smile. "Only that you are the pride of a micco's people and the joy of a father's heart, and I miss you already."

Chapter 3

Two days later

THE BATTLE WAS nothing as I'd imagined.

Even with Iron Wood's warning ringing powerfully through my mind, I'd not grasped the full scope of the destruction that awaited us. Endless showers of musket shot. Bodies piled upon bodies. The stench of blood and defecation. Smoke that stung the eyes and choked the lungs. The chaos of crumbling command.

The ruin of a thousand hopes.

Then again, perhaps, it was the Red Sticks' untainted devotion I had not fully grasped. Their invariable fix on the enemy, on victory. Barring that, on death.

Their, I maintained. *Their* fixation on the enemy, not mine. For when I was not darting to and from the frontline, bags of shot and horns of powder clutched in my sweaty palms, I was kneeling in the dirt clutching my uncle's sightless face to my chest.

I knelt there still, eardrums pummeled by an endless stream of battle cries and musket blasts. The cannon fire had ceased some time ago, having surrendered the notion of penetrating our wall.

Eyes dry, pulse a steady thrum in my neck, I was distantly aware that grief had yet to gain a foothold. I had not allowed it. To succumb was to die. And I could not die until I'd found my warrior's courage.

Far to my left, blue-clad figures surmounted the barrier, flowed over it like a turbulent river. They did not jump from the top onto Red Stick ground but climbed down it on a hill of corpses. Closer to me, some twenty running strides from where I cradled my pawa, another flood of blue surged over the wall.

The force of their rush vibrated through my shins and up my spine. In the next instant, I was on my feet, my pawa lying face-first in a red puddle. The urge to run bit me hard in the thighs. Toward them. From them. I was debating which when a band of warriors twenty-strong streaked past me to meet the foe. One slammed into my shoulder and spun me about to face the onslaught. Tomahawks raised, painted torsos glistening with blood, they shrieked a war cry that raised the hairs on my neck.

The clash deafened, and good sense returning, I crouched where I stood.

"You! Boy!" The shout came at my ear. A pinching grip on my upper arm yanked me around to face a blood-spattered visage. Fierce. Female. A war woman by the tomahawk clutched in her fist. "He wants you. Come!"

"Who wants—"

Her forward haul clacked my jaw shut as she took off at a run. Shoulder nigh yanked from its socket, I stumbled along behind. Tripping over the writhing and the dead, I evaded the worst of the pitted ground.

Seeming assured by my compliance, the war woman released me and focused on her trajectory. Having no other thought but to obey, I followed. Through the fog of gunpowder smoke, I managed to stay on her heels, almost crashing into her when she came to an abrupt halt beside an occupied stretcher.

Without explanation, she leaped over the bloodied fellow and grabbed the unattended carrying poles near his feet. "Go, go!"

A warrior at the stretcher's head squatted and heaved up. In unison, they launched into a precarious jog.

The *zip!* of a musket ball hurdling over my shoulder sent me running after them. *He wants you*, the war woman had said. Did she mean her partner? Injecting speed into my strides, I aimed toward the man. I passed the woman and had nearly caught up when a clamp on my wrist drew my attention down.

From the stretcher, grotto-blue eyes stared up at me from a face painted black with soot. "Fetch her."

I almost missed his words, so focused was I on the stark pallor of the man's lips. "Iron Wood?" A swift assessment down his length to the soggy red bandage high on his thigh told a tale of life slipping away.

"Fetch her to me." His voice rasped with urgency and pain.

"Who?"

"Polly Francis, boy, who else?" the war woman replied, a snap to her panted words. "He will not leave without her, the lovesick fool."

I passed a scowl over my shoulder. What sort of warrior would Iron Wood be if he did? Turning back to Iron Wood, I asked, "Where do I bring her?"

His lashes fluttered shut, then flew wide as the lead carrier hit a rut and bounced the stretcher.

On a grunt, the war woman shifted to balance the load. "The western inlet. Broken cypresses clutter the shore. Do you know it?"

"I do." I'd explored the shore in its entirety only yesterday. That inlet had distinguished itself for the dugout hidden among the tangling vines. "Which lodge will I find her in?" My shouted question rang loud, for the clangor of battle was falling away behind us. The field, too, was clearing of dead and wounded, transitioning to crushed grass.

"The main." Iron Wood peered up at me. Gaze sharp, he seemed to have rallied, at least momentarily, though his jaw trembled as he spoke. "Where she steps, you follow. If she stumbles, you break the fall. If another strikes, you take the blow. Her safety must be all things to you. Say it."

Could a man besiege a boy in such a way? I had never heard it done. But a dying warrior, perhaps, should be granted leeway to demand whatever he wished. And really, what else did I have left to me but the next order to follow?

"*Say it*," Iron Wood scratched out, trembling like a leaf one blow from being stripped from its branch.

"Where she steps, I follow. If she stumbles, I break the fall. If another strikes, I take the blow. Her safety will be all things to me." The words rolled off my tongue with ease. Maybe too much ease. But if the micco's daughter, the future of the People, was not worth dying for, who was?

"Hurry, Water Moccasin." The war woman and her partner picked up speed, and Iron Wood groaned. "Be swift, boy. Do not return without her."

"You will hardly notice me gone." I veered toward the village and choked on that declaration.

Smoke billowed in a poisonous column above the treetops. Dread spidered down my spine. Green pine would not burn so black and dense. But dry lodge-pole thatching would.

Chapter 4

THE <u>CHE-LO-KEES</u>, our ancient enemy, had arrived.

Feet swifting silently over the enclosing forest floor, I aimed for Tohopeka and that toxic black smoke. I arrived on the outskirts in time to see Polly running at full speed into the woods. Toward me, astoundingly, as if to meet partway.

I gave up that notion when she suddenly dipped left, reaching behind dense vegetation, and rose again having snagged a toddler by the arm. With her next stride, she hauled the small body up and flat against her chest.

Iron Wood would not be pleased she'd abandoned her shelter. I, however, was relieved, for she'd saved me a perilous venture into the blazing village.

A shout stopped us both short. I darted behind a covering shrub. Breathing heavily, I stationed myself in a squat and, with a forearm, swiped sweat from my forehead. By the time I peeked out, Polly stood facing the destruction in the clearing.

Every structure burned, a flaming pyre of our noble cause. Che-lo-kee warriors swarmed, herding women and children into the square. The same innocents who'd been assured safety—a forest, a field, and a breastwork manned by a thousand painted males between them and the Bluecoats. Impossible hopes.

Angry heat burned my cheeks. Allies to that cunning dog, General Jackson, the Che-lo-kees seemed to have done the unthinkable and crossed the swollen Tallapoosa. In any other situation, I might admire the feat. In this situation, I admired only their apparent adherence to the white man's practice of not slaughtering helpless ones in the heat of battle. From my position, no child or woman had yet been harmed.

Eyes watering from the smoke, I squinted through the gray haze trapped under the thick, leafy canopy above. Fists clenched in the child's tunic, Polly appeared frozen with indecision. Black ash smudged her face, a war mask for the fight that awaited us. But first, she must join me. Ten strides more and she'd be at my side. Precisely where I needed her.

The soles of my feet itched to fly to the woman, but if I could lure her this way, so much the better. "Polly," I whisper-shouted, but the roaring flames ate up my panted words. "Polly Francis." A little louder.

Not a twitch of her head, though the child—no older than three winters—twisted to see behind her. Dirt patched her face, and tears glistened in her eyes. I waved frantically, but she merely blinked at me, her plump lips agape.

On a huff of frustration, I dug into my pouch for the signaling metal my pawa had given me at the war's start. In the time since the battle began, the sun had burned a substantial trail across the <u>Upper World</u>, but there was enough light to catch and use. Angling the instrument, I flashed a beam into Polly's side vision.

Slamming that eyelid shut, she veered from the nuisance, then cautiously glanced back. She spotted me, her lips turning down with confusion before she gave her head a firm shake. Scooping at the air, she called me to her.

I wagged my head vehemently and replicated her gathering motion, urging her my direction.

She looked back toward the dying village, but the warriors had no interest in the surrounding woodland. A sign they had already infiltrated and secured it. Fortunately, inside this sector of shadowed woods, all was yet still.

Sight darting about, she finally began toward me. Ten long strides had her crouched at my left, the girlchild straddling her hip. "Have you lost all sanity?" she hissed. "Put that mirror away!"

Yes, I had. For having so haphazardly taken on a vow to protect a micco's daughter, one who wore a dagger sheathed at her waist and commanded men as if she were a micco herself. In the end, who would be protecting whom?

Something cracked behind her. A flintlock? Both our heads whipped around, but the forest seemed empty.

I continued panning, all the while heaving for breath. Sweat ran a tickling path down my neck and over my shirtless chest. Here I was dripping perspiration to retrieve the woman for her betrothed yet receiving only a reprimand for my efforts. "Aren't you a...firebolt."

"Says the rabbit kitten who doesn't know when to stop playing warrior."

That swung my head back to her. Our eyes clicked, and hers were...

My brows jogged up my forehead. I canted in for a closer look. Bright blue flecked her hazel irises in a stunning collage.

The scowl etching into her features snapped me out of my distraction. Regathering my senses and my sense of urgency, I drew back. "Iron Wood sent me. He's wounded and cannot come for you as promised."

She blanched. "Is it bad?"

Worse than bad. Not that I would say as much. "Bullet to the thigh. Prophet Francis bids him escape. But your man, he will not leave unless you're with him. I swore I would find you. Follow me." Without waiting for even a nod of understanding, I clawed onto her upper arm and tugged her upright with me.

The child fussed and clung fiercely to Polly's disheveled hair, but Polly either didn't care or, in her shock, didn't feel it. Satisfied the woman would follow, I picked up speed.

We sailed through the underbrush. The distant clamor of war, the flash of the sun through the treetops—they were little more than a blur in my subconscious. All I knew was Iron Wood and my vow, Polly and her rhythmic stride beside my own.

Cutting around obstacles, leaping others, tearing through creepers and prickly vines, we barreled through the woods. Straight toward the swampy cove I'd come across not two sleeps earlier.

Nearing the spot, I slowed to a crawl, ear cocking this way and that, listening for any sign of enemy presence. Not a simple task, considering the noisome river. It coursed around a rocky bend, splashing and gurgling on our right. I heard nothing alarming, and nearby foliage did not appear disturbed.

Appeased, I picked up my pace, soon reaching a fallen long-leaf pine propped high off the ground by its dead branches. I pushed a flowering shrub aside, far enough to allow Polly to duck under the tree. Toes squelching into boggy soil, we pushed through the greenery and into an inlet sheltered on three sides. A ring of boulders, cypress stumps, and the fallen pine acted as decent coverage.

A single dugout waited empty at the water's edge. Beside it, on a dry hump of ground, Iron Wood sat propped against a cypress knee, one leg bloodied and bound up tight, the other sunk in silty water. At his sides were the war woman and her stretcher-carrying companion.

"Polly!" Bloody fingers outstretched, Iron Wood beckoned.

Even across the distance, I noted the quake of his limbs, the wobble of his head as he struggled to keep it upright. Lips washed of all color, he sweated a river to match the Tallapoosa. The amount of blood soaking his legging staggered me. High on his thigh, the wound was too near that vital artery. Would the man make it off this bank alive?

Polly's thoughts, perhaps, ran the same course, for she stood and stared at her man.

"Polly?" Iron Wood's blinks fell sluggish, confused, mere beats from not lifting again.

From behind, I gave her a brusque nudge to snap her back into herself. Choking on a cry, she splashed a hurried trail through the shallows. "I'm here, I'm here!"

"Finally." The war woman directed her glowering brow at me. "Thought you were done for, boy." She wasted no time squeezing her small but sturdy frame behind Iron Wood, then hooking her hands in the pits of his arms.

Polly jogged onto the scene, while the war woman's companion—Water Moccasin, I recalled—reached for Iron Wood's legs, blocking her access to him. He and the war woman heaved, and Iron Wood groaned as he left the ground.

Uttering a forced laugh, Polly scratched out a spate of English mildly reproachful in tone, to which Iron Wood gave a slurring reply. Lids shut, he stuck his tongue out at her.

Their banter squeezed me somewhere under the ribs, and I couldn't decide if it was yearning or...something less admirable. A single laugh sobbed from her then, and shame averted my eyes. I tuned my ears to the sobering gunfire filtering through the trees until Polly began moving again. Patted the little bottom perched on her forearm, she followed close to the warriors as they hustled toward the dugout, Iron Wood's limp form swinging between them.

The vessel was narrow, room enough for two, certainly not three. Either the war woman or Water Moccasin would be swimming alongside.

"That plank there," she said to me, gesturing wildly. "Fetch it, will you? Be quick!"

Ah, excellent idea. Without cover on the dugout, they would never manage to get the craft beyond the soldiers. Dozens were likely camped along the river, rifles primed to pick off any who fled.

While the silent Water Moccasin arranged a groaning Iron Wood on his side in the dugout, the war woman traipsed over to help me. Together, we freed the slab of half-rotted wood from beneath several others, then laid it over the dugout, sheltering Iron Wood's torso.

I stepped back out of the way while Polly, speaking Muscogee now, stroked the damp hair back from her man's face. "How is that? Comfortable? Stable enough?"

"Mmm, fine," he garbled through pressed, death-white lips.

Hand on Iron Wood's shoulder, she looked to the war woman. "My father?"

Water Moccasin bent for a paddle, but the war woman met the inquiry head-on. "Shot."

Polly's lower lip trembled. "Dead?"

"Shot many times."

"So, he is dead?"

"Three, four wounds, maybe more."

"Is he *dead*." Polly gritted the demand between her teeth, and I understood how it was an army of men could look to her as miccohokti.

Why did the war woman not wish to reply? She stared at Polly, face an unreadable slate of stone. "I cannot say. He fell."

"They could be flesh wounds."

And her father was a prophet who communed with spirits. Of all men on the field, he should be most protected.

"Who is that you have?" Iron Wood's voice was a mere rasp.

"Cricket," Polly replied on a stroke of the child's hair.

"I can...take her." He patted the gap between his body and the wall of the dugout.

Polly gazed at the girl who squealed and made grasping motions at Iron Wood. Had the child no living family? No clan?

Apparently not, for Polly finally said, "All right, Cricket. You can go." She released the child to wiggle beneath the plank covering Iron Wood. In moments, Cricket was nestling against his side. Half-conscious, he curled his body around her. "But you must lie very, very still," Polly said. "His leg hurts. Do not bump it, and if you raise your head, the ride will be over."

In answer, Cricket squirmed close to Iron Wood and babbled in his ear.

"I'll...keep her down."

"Of course, and you, Mr. Bellamy,"—she caught a leafy vine the war woman flung overtop the plank—"no English heroics. Lay there and rest. On top of Cricket if she doesn't stop wiggling." Polly's laugh came out slightly manic.

The war woman sank thigh-deep in the water, grabbed the vine from under the dugout, and wrapped it again—a shoddy tie-down and perhaps a hope they would pass for floating debris.

Polly crouched low and shared furtive, urgent words with Iron Wood. Intimate words not meant for me. I eased farther back onto the boggy shore and stayed clear of their business. My work was finished, after all.

"Done," Water Moccasin announced over the knot he tied into the vine's ends. "We must move."

Polly nodded and backed away, gaze pasted to a now-unconscious Iron Wood.

"Get in the dugout, Polly." That was the war woman.

"I cannot leave my father to bleed out." Polly took a step back. Toward me. "If there is a chance to help him, I must take it."

No, she mustn't, but who was I to tell her so? If my father lay dying and I had the opportunity to help him, I would do the same. On that thought, I curled my lips in and pinched them between my teeth.

The war woman tried again. "Micco Crazy Medicine ordered us to—"

"Was I included in that order?"

"Not specifically, but you are—"

"Then you and your brother will take my betrothed to safety. As the micco ordered."

The war woman glared at her, and Polly returned it, their eyes locked in a battle of wills. At last, the strict line of the war woman's mouth softened. She tipped her chin sideways, head lowering in a bow. "Very well, Polly."

That was it then, the extension of my vow. Whether she wanted me or not, Polly would have me along. We would search out her father, then her betrothed. Only then would my vow be complete.

The women were still speaking, and I was missing it. I edged closer, engaged now that it was my future they planned.

"He went down on the far eastern side of the wall," the war woman said. "Wait until the end. If he is going to live through his wounds, he will do so whether you arrive before the bullets have stopped flying or after. Do not risk your life needlessly, or he will lift my scalp. Then I will lift yours." Her lips peeled back in a ferocious baring of the teeth before she reeled about and shoved the vessel into the water. "Have a care for your life, daughter of the prophet. And when you see him, tell him I have his Englishman safe with me, and we will meet in the Floridas. Where we discussed."

"I will. Keep him alive. And Mink?" When the woman glanced back, Polly continued, tone replete with promise. "If he begins his spirit journey, it will be me you answer to."

Mink, as she'd been called, grinned. "Understood, little she-wolf."

I'd forgotten Polly was Wolf Clan, a fact that explained her intensely protective nature. I could appreciate such a character trait. Even as Rabbit. So long as she didn't bite my head off for insisting on staying at her side, we should get along.

Water Moccasin bid her farewell with an embrace and a word of encouragement, then he and Mink were shoving off, neither boarding but sinking up to their noses in the water, guiding the craft into the river's exuberant flow. With them went any steadiness Polly could boast. Her legs wobbled first, arms trembling slightly at her sides. Even the wolf, it seemed, could tremble.

I sidled up and clasped her shaking palm in mine. "Do not watch."

Polly startled as if having forgotten I existed, but in the next moment she leaned in, giving me some of her weight. I gladly bore it, pleased I could be of some use.

"Will he make it, do you think?" she whispered.

I would not reply with anything other than the truth, but she didn't seem to want that. So I said nothing. She didn't press for a lie, only leaned harder.

For the next short while, we tracked the dugout as it rocked and hurdled through the swells. Too soon, I felt compelled to move and gave her hand an urging tug. "Come, look away. Look to your father." I peered up at her then and, frowning, swiped a finger along her cheekbone. I hadn't known she was crying, and the sight pinched my heart.

For many breaths, as warm water lapped at our ankles, she stood watching the place we'd last seen the dugout. But we could not delay.

"Polly."

Her lashes, weighted with droplets, lowered and lifted before she dragged her sight to me. Her ribs expanded. Her shoulder blades pulled together. Her chin lifted a degree. The wolf coming awake.

"Well done, Polly. Look to living," I said on a nod, admiration warming my bones.

I coaxed her around and set my jaw, gaze drilling toward the field of combat and the gore that awaited us.

"Living might be a stretch," she said, "even for a child's hope. I'll content myself with surviving, maddo."

"Stop that," I clipped at once, swinging my attention back to her. Never mind she'd called me a child. That defeatist spirit would not do. Not in my company. "We will *live*. Together."

Or fall together, for if another struck at her, I'd take the blow. But I wouldn't let either happen. I had too much life to live. To begin with, I had my pawa's dream of a reborn Alabama Town to fulfill.

Wrinkles forming across her brow, she gave her head a slow shake.

"Do not think you will go without me." My voice was flint now. "Where you step, I will follow, and that is the end of it."

A snort of air puffed from her nose.

"Well?" I demanded. If she mocked me or my purpose, I would have to set the micco's daughter straight.

Her lips twitched at the corners as she ran her sight across my face and bare chest, pausing on my clan tattoo. "What are you called, little rabbit kit?"

Though tempted to grind my teeth, I let the diminutive roll off me. Who but this *kit* had brought the wolf from the brink of despair? In my deepest voice, I replied, "True Seeker."

"What is it you seek?"

"As of this moment, you. And whatever it is *you* seek."

Her mouth puckered at what had to seem an odd attachment, but after a moment's consideration, she dipped her chin. "All right, then, Kit. Together."

Chapter 5

FROM THE INLET where we'd watched the dugout slip away, Polly and I set out through the woods at a jog, uncaring we might be heard despite the battle clamor having dimmed to the occasional spattering of musket shot. The forest lay empty, every man focused on defending the breastwork that was each moment less Red Stick more Bluecoat.

Undeterred by the spine-chilling sounds of battle, Polly clutched her skirt in two fists and ran slightly ahead of me. Long and lean, her legs navigated the undergrowth with ease as she cut through the trees. She flew like an arrow in her father's direction. To find him. Save him. Our first glimpse of the field told us both how farfetched that idea had been.

Polly burst from the tree line and took three steps before her legs gave way. Then her stomach emptied itself, splattering its contents on a carpet of dead pine needles.

At her side, I stopped short and surveyed the terrain. The structural integrity of my own knees coming swiftly into question. When I'd left a short while ago, the day had been all but won. The victor all but declared. Even so, I had not viewed the grounds from this angle. Had not seen the full scope of the devastation.

"They are gone," Polly croaked, voice unrecognizable. Then she heaved again.

My stomach quivered and lurched as though answering her call. Swallowing hard, I steeled it against revolt. I knelt at Polly's side and pushed the words through my clotted throat. "They are." I brushed windblown hair back from her wet mouth, but my eyes would not quit the field.

One thousand warriors. Strewn across the land the length of the wall. Piled atop one another like a child's stick-fort kicked down by the wind and trampled. Bone. Flesh. Innards. Exposed as they should not be. No death had been neatly met.

That morning, the thousand had been alive, unconquerable. Now, to a man, they were broken and split open, left to bleed out as if they were cattle at slaughter. And the blood... Puddles, ponds, downhill streams. The ground bogged with it.

The only activity came from Blue-coated soldiers who swarmed the area. Some climbed the bulwark. Some sat upon it, bodies slumped, as they caught their wind. Or gaped at the devastation same as myself. Some fought the final resilient few. On the other side, others hacked at the wall with axes while horses, mounted by straight-backed figures, waited for access.

None looked our way, or did and skipped over us.

When Polly's stomach at last expended itself, she raised her head and stared out across the battlefield. Tears magnified the gray of her eyes. Wet skipped down her cheeks and dropped from her chin. "He slaughtered them all," she said at last, tone dead.

He. General Jackson. That old, sharp knife. The one that dug between the People's ribs and carved out our hearts, then trampled our lands, claiming it with bloody boot prints. When would he stop?

Never was the truth carried by the smoke-scented wind. *Never*.

So then. Who would stop him? Every man on these grounds had wished to. Courage large in their hearts, they'd tried to. For their efforts, they were either gone the way of Iron Wood or gone the way of Keeps Watch Hardjo. None remained to carry out the deed. None but we.

Polly gathered her skirt and made to rise, so I hooked her under the arm to assist. When she stood, it was on unsteady legs and with a beautiful silver blade clutched in a white-knuckled grip.

I eyed it. Eyed her.

She eyed me. Eyed the gory field.

It occurred to me to tell her to put it away, to not draw trouble, but I stayed my tongue. When facing Bluecoats, every person was entitled to self-protection.

Needles crunching beneath my moccasins, I sidled closer. "Are you certain?"

She dipped a slow nod. "To my father."

My stomach pitched. The hand I extended to her trembled, but once enveloped by her own shaky hand, it steadied. Resolve settled within me. "To your father. To whatever end this day holds."

We began an aimless wander across the corpse-cluttered expanse, checking faces, searching, searching. Red liquid filled into the indents left by our treads, seeped through the seams of my moccasins, and wet the spaces between my toes.

Despair pressed down, but hunger gnawing and Polly weeping, we searched on.

In time, Grandmother Sun's weakening rays glowed ruddy on the faces of the last of the Bluecoat soldiers sedately scaling the wall. Confident in their ownership of the day, they waded through the dead and dying.

I adhered to Polly like stickseed, my only weapon the daggers of my eyes, which I hurled at every soldier who took a second glance our way. Clutched to each other, with Polly keening unabashedly, we created an image of grieving innocents. It served us well. A few soldiers rattled English at us. Each time, Polly found the coherence to respond. Though to me it was but gibberish, they invariably allowed us to go where we willed. Fools, the lot of them.

As the war woman had instructed, we covered the far eastern sector where she'd said Crazy Medicine fell. Not a downed man—most dead, a few dying—escaped our scrutiny, but we did not find the one we sought. Though weary, we trekked the length of the zigzag wall, expanding our search until my feet stuttered to a halt beside a familiar face.

Polly joined me in gazing down on the warrior's pallid visage. "Nokose Fixico," she said, voice lifeless. "You knew him?"

I lowered a somber nod. "An old friend of my pawa's. Another gone." One more loss to add to the tally. One less man to help gather whatever remained of the People and begin anew.

"I am not dead...yet, young Rabbit," the man groaned from between the crack in his lips. His lashes fluttered, then lifted to half-staff. "Only broken."

My pulse leaped. "Nokose!" I dropped to a knee and, skipping a glance down his seemingly intact length, took up his frigid, lifeless hand. "Where are you wounded? What can I do?"

"My back," he ground out.

At a nod from me, Polly jumped over Nokose to his other side, revealing the hilt of a second, smaller blade tucked into her ankle-high moccasin. The woman carried two blades, and I carried none. Yet I was the named protector? Shame dealt me a glancing blow. What true purpose had I served here on this field?

"Help me roll him, True Seeker," she said, drawing me back from my self-deprecation.

Together, we eased Nokose onto his side. I held him steady as Polly bent to assess. In moments, she met my eyes, her mouth stretching into a thin line that said nothing and everything at the same time.

"Well?" Nokose demanded. "Give it to me plain."

"You are not bleeding out but..." She eased him back down and looked the warrior straight on. "A ball is lodged in your spine and appears to have broken it."

Defeat sank through me, reaching unseen depths. The same appeared to crash over Nokose. His lashes fell. He exhaled a lungful of air, then opened his eyes and formed a meager smile. "That would explain the dead limbs. I feel nothing."

A shudder coursed through me at the prospect of paralysis, but there was mercy in it. "What...what can we do?" I asked once more, though I knew the answer.

"Nothing, young Rabbit. Nothing."

Yes. That answer.

"Except..." Nokose gazed steadily into the orange-streaked sky. "My wife is here at Tohopeka. Singing Grass, she is called." At the voicing of her name, that miserable smile of his firmed around the edges, his gaze shifting into a realm of memories where I could not follow.

"I know her." Polly took up his other hand and clutched it high where he could see. "You have a message?"

"I have sung my death song," he replied as though not hearing. Perhaps, he hadn't. Perhaps, he'd already stepped foot on the spirit road. "My life is done, but Singing Grass will come shortly in search. She must not see me in such a state. Broken and unmendable as I am."

My throat bobbed with a convulsive swallow, but Polly, collected and steady, did not flinch. She passed a soothing palm over his forehead. "She will not, brother, for we will not abandon you to your brokenness."

Water accumulated in Nokose's dulling eyes. "Maddo, daughter of Francis."

"Pah. For your sacrifice, it is a little thing I do."

She would take the task upon herself then? Should I allow it or spare her that burden?

"Tell me, though," she went on, "have you seen my father? We have searched but—"

Nokose was already shaking his head. Tiny, abrupt movements. "He is gone. Taken away."

"Taken? By whom?" She cut me a glance, fear ripe in her sky-flecked eyes.

"By ours?" I asked and did not breathe again until Nokose affirmed.

"Yes." The syllable hissed over the man's sluggish tongue.

"Where? Where, Nokose? Do you know?" Excitement pitched Polly's voice high as she canted sharply over him, but when he muttered an apologetic denial, she was quick to resume stroking his head. "It is all right, it is all right. You have helped."

"Good," he breathed the word. "I am a Muscogee warrior. I am not afraid to die."

"I see no fear in you, my friend." Smiling into his face, she discreetly stationed her blade's tip over his heart. "You are ready, then?"

Damp flooded my palm. I should offer to do it. "Polly," I began, but with a jerk of the chin, she cut me off. I eased back, giving her space.

Tongue passing over bloodless lips, Nokose seemed to rally strength. Polly waited, and though he couldn't feel it, I tightened my grip on his hand and wished desperately I was not there. Wished I could dart to my feet and run until their soles were bloodied. Until the cool, dark interior of my mother's lodge embraced me.

But I could not dart or run or even look away. For honor's sake, I could do nothing but fight the painful lump in my throat and thank the spirits I was not the one fisting that blade. Did that make me a coward or simply a peace-loving <u>White Stick</u> at heart? I did not know.

At last, voice firm, Nokose said, "I am ready."

"Then I bid you go with Spirit." Shifting her weight, Polly leaned into her dagger. Its fine silver point slipped soundlessly through flesh and between bone and found a home deep in the warrior's chest. Before he could try for his next breath, she slid the blade free to let his blood spill and mingle in the earth with that of his brothers.

That next breath never came. Resigned, Nokose emptied his lungs, blinked once more, and set out on the journey.

We had our own journey to complete. So, while Polly chanted a final prayer, I lowered his eyelids and wiped her blade on the grass. While I folded his arms across his chest, Polly stilled me with a touch to my elbow, then brushed my hands away and fingered the leather-cord bracelet Nokose wore. From it dangled a tiny set of sticks, the shorter tied crossways to the longer, both painted red. She stared at it, mouth hanging at a slight part.

"What does it mean?"

Her teeth clicked shut. From between them, she seethed, "The symbol of the white man's Great Spirit named Jesus."

My eyebrows shot up. "Nokose worshiped Creator in the manner of the whites?"

"Why else would he wear this?" She flicked the pendant, sending it spinning on its cord.

Why else, indeed. But... "Does it matter?"

Eyes cutting to me, Polly dispensed a barbed look. "Does it matter!"

"Iron Wood wears a medicine pouch. Nokose wore a Jesus symbol." I shrugged.

The tension around her eyes softened. "What are you saying?"

"Each must answer to Creator on his own. Who are we to judge?" I pushed to my feet, laying a hand to her shoulder. "We must go. The fight isn't finished." As if I'd spoken conjury, the sounds of battle rushed back in. Louder, more intense than it had been. Shouting, sporadic blasts.

Forehead tightening, I rotated toward the commotion. Taking it in, I gripped Polly's arm. "Look.

There." I stretched my arm, her sight following. "A few remain."

The last resistance, a pocket of fighting warriors had holed up at a well-defended angle of the zigzag bulwark, right in the crook of a deep V. Hidden behind hastily collected logs and brush, they could not be reached but neither could they escape. From my perspective, they were breathing their last.

Around the entrenched warriors, Bluecoats had positioned themselves in an arch, some kneeling, some prone, some concealed by improvised barricades. Most were a blur of blue coats and white faces. Some were slightly more remarkable.

But for the sketch Iron Wood had pinned to the table before me, I might not have recognized the mounted Bluecoat orchestrating a one-sided negotiation. Bushy white hair seated his two-cornered hat. The yellow trim of a stiff blue collar cut a line across his jaw, and gold tassels danced on his shoulders. Then there were his eyes: piercing, keen, pale blue. No drawing could have captured them, but their commanding slice across the field confirmed to me at once who we'd stumbled across: Old Sharp Knife Jackson.

Chapter 6

AS POLLY STARED at the general, she wondered, not for the first time or the dozenth, how much her father had foreseen. Whether he'd known Old Sharp Knife and Polly's fates would collide.

Straddling a tall dappled-gray mare, General Jackson brazenly faced his barricaded foes. A small army of foot soldiers spread out to each side, crouching behind anything serviceable as cover.

Through a White Stick Muscogee interpreter, who perched high on his own horse beside the white chief, the two-tongued general attempted dialogue, calling out promises of life and humane treatment. "You must put down the fight," the interpreter hollered, "give yourselves up!"

Their reply came in the form of a musket blast that blew the White Stick traitor from his horse. He landed face-down in the mud and did not move. If they'd been aiming for the general, the miss was not disappointing.

A cackle cut from Polly's throat. Jackson was a stupid boar to have thought they would surrender that easily. Her fingers ached to wrap around his throat.

True Seeker pulled urgently on her arm, shouting words she could not hear over the sound of her deranged laughter and the soldiers' deafening return fire. Even after the volley ended, she heard nothing but the victory whoop howling in her mind, saw nothing but the general heeling his mare, wheeling the animal around behind the shelter of a stout oak—a move that put him directly in Polly's line of sight.

Prophecy coming at her in force, Polly ran out of laughter.

Her vision blackened at the edges until all she saw was the beast who'd heartlessly denied the People their land and torn their lives apart with his own hands. Though muskets fired again and True Seeker spoke, she noted only the wind, its direction and speed. Felt only the spring of her muscles as she burst into a run. Tasted only the sweet cup of vengeance.

Flipping her father's dagger, she pinched it by its pointed tip. In the next instant, she raised her arm and hurled the blade.

There was her grunt of exertion, the abrupt halt of her race, a soldier's too-late bark of warning, then the bone-cracking impact of failure. Jackson's bicorne sailed off his gray head, the flash of silver right behind it, flipping end over end.

The brute barely flinched. Just turned his eyes on Polly. Sharp blue, those eyes. Cold. Stormy. Altogether terrifying.

They froze her, and she knew she was done. The half-dozen rifles swiveling her way, clinched it.

Pain slammed into her, kicked her off her feet. The back of her skull bounced off the soft earth. After, nothing but an orange-streaked evening sky and agony.

A wail built within, fed less by the hot ball buried in her shoulder, more by the anguish of defeat. Teeth clamped fast, she locked it away. As if coaxing her to join in, the moans and death rattles of wounded men sounded on every side, her own restrained only by her dying pride. These Bluecoats might have witnessed her disgrace on that acreage of desecrated meadow, but they would not hear the regret of it.

"Polly!" True Seeker crashed to his knees at her side. Nostrils blown wide, he appeared above her. He slapped both hands to her wound, one atop the other, and expressed a groan from her throat. "Terrible shot, just terrible." He sketched a wobbly smile that breathed a trickle of life into her dying spirits.

"You could have," she said, panting through the pain, "done better?"

"Ask me later."

"The...damage?"

"Bad enough that Iron Wood will have sharp words for you."

No, Iron Wood would not speak to her of this. Even if they both survived their injuries, her neck would not survive its stretching. Polly shook her head, tears streaming into her ears. "Iron Wood is—"

"Alive and waiting for you downriver. I intend to see you get there. Now, shut up and disarm before the soldiers arrive." Indeed, the pound of boots, or perhaps hooves, reverberated through the ground and traveled into her bones. "There are better ways to gain an audience with the white chief, you know," True Seeker added with another flimsy smile.

Coughing out an incredulous laugh, Polly worked trembling fingers around the small paring blade sheathed to her waist. Knife freed, she tucked it under the knee pressed to her side. He recognized it with a nod, but when a soldier trotted up, squatted at her other side, and reached as if to touch her, the weapon True Seeker wielded wasn't the knife. Rising on his knees, he landed his fist squarely on the fellow's nose, spraying red.

Taken wholly off guard, the Bluecoat fell back on his seat, a garbled cry issuing from between the fingers covering his face.

Snarling, True Seeker followed his fist's momentum and stretched half atop her, one leg twining tightly about hers as if to say, *you take one, you take both*. As though his scrawny body would be any deterrent to the hundred and more soldiers gathering for a glimpse of the woman crazy enough to attack their highest chief.

Blood gushed from the soldier's slit cheekbone but was no deterrent to the threats and profanities issuing from him in a constant stream. Or to the counterattack that slammed a fist into True Seeker's nose.

His head whipped sideways, blood an instant fountain, but he was not moved from his place atop her. Indeed, he gripped her harder, face tucked against her and shoulders hunched.

Another voice, muffled by the blood pounding in Polly's ears, entered her sphere. "I've seen you before, private, and I daresay you deserved that. Stand down."

Judging by the soldier's scramble and the speed with which he gulped down his swears, the new arrival could only be General Jackson. He stalked to where they were and for a long, agonizing minute stood with hands clasped behind him and peered down his aquiline nose at her. Assessing. Judging. Deciding their fate.

Polly lay mouth open and panting like a winded dog while True Seeker bodily covered her and whispered trembling assurances in her ear: she would live, he would make it so, the general would receive his due, the spirits would make it so. She listened with half an ear, gritted her teeth against the hot poker digging under her collar bone, and affixed half-lidded eyes to Old Sharp Knife.

"The girl threw the knife, you say, not the boy?" He looked her dead in the eye. Someone answered in the affirmative, and one of his gray eyebrows jogged up. "A noble attempt, young lady." His tone was a stomach-turning mixture of admiration and taunting. "But you missed."

She collected saliva and lobbed it onto his boot. The one wet with the blood of her people. Baring her teeth at him, she ground Muskogee between them. "I would be pleased to try again."

More voices, more questions, all muffled by the roaring inside her head, then he smirked. "Plucky little thing, I'll give her that." In her pain, the world smeared and ran together, but then Sharp Knife said,

"Absolutely not, Captain. She's had punishment enough. Patch her up. If she survives, put her with the rest of the captives."

Patch her— What? Did he mean to let her live?

Punishment enough, the general had said.

Captives lived. In time, were released.

Breath sighed from her lungs. To the best of her ability, she'd done as her father bid, as the prophecy demanded. Though, what the point of it all had been—apart from damaging her and her faithful companion—she didn't know. True Seeker's weight and warmth pressed into her like a comforting blanket. The blood from his smashed nose soaked her blouse and merged with her own. In blood and bondage, they were in this together, and she was grateful not to be alone.

With her next inhale, Iron Wood flitted into her mind, his bright eyes smiling, and suddenly, all she wanted was him. Pain thrumming through her, she reached for hope and found it as peace and darkness began a creeping sweep across her vision.

"Well done, Polly," came True Seeker's voice, distant through the encroaching black. "Rest now. I will see the future secured."

"Maddo." The word passed over her tongue on a whisper, then she surrendered to sleep, her last thoughts these: the general didn't know he looked upon the daughter of his most excellent enemy, and True Seeker spoke no English.

~ ~ ~

"Polly? Polly!" I pressed a frantic palm to her chest. At the faithful thump of her heart, the air whooshed from my lungs, relief sweeping in to take its place.

But what did it matter that her heart had not quit? The woman already forfeited her life. She might as well have buried that dagger in her own temple.

Grief clogged my throat, nearly cutting off my wind. In this, I had failed Iron Wood.

But it was not a complete loss.

Where it concerned Old Sharp Knife, my mettle was yet untested. And he was there, *right there*. As was Polly's small blade. It dug into my kneecap where it hid against her side, begging to be put to use. To make this terrible day, this senseless slaughter, and the Red Sticks' sacrifice count for something. Something more than proof we were Muscogee and not afraid to die.

Drop him where he stands. Iron Wood's voice came back at me, riding the myriad groans that hovered the dying field like an <u>Under World</u> fog and seeped into my skin. *The Americans will choose him...then he will move on to remove other nations. Any who stands in his path will be sliced down.*

Drop the white chief. End the oppression. Had any other Red Stick been presented a riper opportunity? Doubtful. And had we not all come to Horse's Flat Foot to die? My pawa's dream of a new Alabama Town would have to pass to another.

Drop him.

I would.

The knife's handle bit into my bone.

I will.

Heart thundering against my ribs, I stayed as I was, bent over Polly, my weight bearing down on the stack of my hands. The iron ball that knocked her off her feet bulged into my palm where I compressed her wound.

Drop him! Before he dropped me.

"The ball should be dug out." The words fell from between my numb lips. For whoever cared to understand. "Best to do it while she sleeps." Not awaiting a response, I fished the paring knife from under my knee. Hand shaking violently, I wiped its dusty blade on my thigh and lifted the blood-soaked compress, using the pretense of assessing the wound.

A gift of the spirits, Old Sharp Knife lowered to a squat at Polly's opposite side. Uttering a quiet stream of English, he angled closer, as though begging for a finger's length of steel in his jugular. Gaze fixed to that pulsing blood vessel, I held the knife low, turning it in my palm for an efficient downward strike. My muscles had only just coiled for the blow when cold fingers found my wrist and clamped on.

Polly. Those blue-flecked eyes locked on me through the droop of their lashes. Her tongue emerged to lay down moisture before she wheezed, "Mercy."

A tiny growl escaped me. "He does not deserve—"

"For us. He has said...mercy."

The wind caught in my throat.

Mercy. For us? For Polly? Was that possible? I lifted my gaze to the Old Sharp Knife and jolted at the spear of his ice-blue study. Of me. Of the tiny blade trembling in my clutches. He did not appear of a merciful nature. "Are you...certain you heard right, Polly?" Through the pain. Through the rage.

"Yes." The word hissed from between her slack lips. "Each must answer...to Creator on his own. Let it...go."

My fingers eased open, and the knife fell to the waist of her skirt. The general slipped the weapon into the holder on his blood-stained boot and straightened his knees. With a slow nod for me and an abrupt word for Polly, he turned and left us, taking with him my chance to make a difference.

Regret sliced at me, tears pricking the backs of my lids. I should have acted without hesitation. I should have killed the monster. I should have laid open his vein and rid the world of his—

Polly laced our fingers and pulled them to rest against her heart. The organ beat erratically against the back of my hand, an apt reminder of my vow. More than vengeance, more than justice, her safety was all things to me. Where she stepped, I would follow. Even into captivity. A more trying feat, perhaps, than dying.

Courage was nothing as I'd imagined.

Squeezing my fingers into hers, I leaned near and showed her my smiling wet eyes. "Very well, Polly Francis. We will *live*. Together."

Thank you for reading *We Are Come to Die!*

For the continuation of True Seeker's story,
read *The Ebony Cloak.*

For Mink's romance, read *Love the War Woman.*

For True Seeker and Polly's romance,
read *Finding Pretty Wolf.*

For Water Moccasin's romance,
read *Strike of the Water Moccasin.*

About the Author

APRIL W GARDNER is an award-winning indie author. Her great passion is historical romance with themes of Native American and Southeastern U.S. culture. Copyeditor, mother of two grown children, and non-trad college student, April lives in South Texas with her husband and two German Shepherds.

Enjoy these other books by April:
HISTORICAL FICTION

Beneath the Blackberry Moon parts 1-3
(must be read in order)
The Red Feather
The Sacred Writings
The Ebony Cloak
The Untold Stories

Drawn by the Frost Moon
(standalones)
Bitter Eyes No More
Love the War Woman
Finding Pretty Wolf
Strike of the Water Moccasin
We Are Come to Die

STANDALONE ROMANCE
Beautiful in His Sight
Better than Fiction

MIDDLE GRADE HISTORICAL FICTION
Lizzie and the Guernsey Gang

BIBLE COMMENTARY/BIBLICAL FICTION
A Hope Fulfilled (novella)
Knowing Obadiah (commentary)
But in Mount Zion (Bible study)

WRITING RESOURCE
Body Beats to Build On, a Fiction Writer's Resource

Connect with April online at:
www.aprilgardner.com
info@aprilgardner.com
facebook.com/april.gardner1

Visit aprilgardner.com and
subscribe to receive a free novel.

Author's Note and Acknowledgements

This has been a year (2022) for breaking the mold. *Strike of the Water Moccasin* was a first for me in several ways. First short novel (57K). First with one POV. First all-male POV. *We Are Come to Die* has its own firsts. First novella (17K). First story written in first person.

Being a full-time college kid has forced me to adapt, and I'm not unhappy with the changes. I hope you're enjoying the variety as much as I am.

As mentioned at the beginning of the book, this story was written as a college assignment. One of the requirements was that I had to give it an anti-colonial angle, not a difficult task when considering the settings of my books. I admit that, as a white woman, it was straight-up hard. Writing so bluntly about the atrocities committed by whites against the indigenous people of the United States was not pleasant.

And that's considering I've been writing about it for well over a decade already. This battle, though, is another level. It's an uncomfortable topic altogether, but there's no getting around the ugliness of our nation's history or of the abuses of those in power.

Once the semester project was completed, I participated in a symposium where we explained our project to the class. I'll share part of it with you here...

Troubles for the Muscogees, the tribe that controlled present-day Alabama, began in 1813 with the Creek War [as portrayed in *The Red Feather*]. Their year-long war with the Americans was their protest against the incursion of settlers on their land. They lost that war in the most tragic way, which is depicted in the story I've written for this course.

It's set during the Battle of Horseshoe Bend, also called Horse's Flat Foot. It took place in March of 1814 in what is now southern Alabama. It's the last, decisive battle of the Creek War in which 1,000 Muscogee warriors took a final stand. Because they would not surrender, only a handful survived. One of the men responsible for that bloody battle was also the cause of the Trail of Tears: General Andrew Jackson, later President Andrew Jackson.

Before he reached office, General Jackson used the Creek War to wrest most of the land from the Muscogees. He's also responsible for the brutal annihilation of Negro Fort [as portrayed in *The Ebony Cloak*]. After that, he conducted an unlawful invasion of Spanish Florida during the First Seminole War while chasing down the last Muscogee resisters from the Creek War [Drawn by the Frost Moon series].

In 1839, his first year in office as president, he signed into effect the Indian Removal Policy, which displaced indigenous tribes from all across the Southeast and Midwest, including Cherokees, Chickasaws, Choctaws, Seminoles, Muscogees, and many others. The estimated number of displacements from these named tribes alone was 60,000. Of the Muscogees, there were approximately 3,500 deaths on the forced march west.

My parents raised me to respect our nation's leaders, but some make it rather difficult, Andrew Jackson being one of them. I'm veering dangerously close to political talk here (thanks for your indulgence!), and that is not my calling. I do, however, always strive to reveal hidden parts of American history. This battle, though not exactly unknown, is often overlooked for the more notable battles of the War of 1812, which was concurrent with the Creek War.

It's my prayer that through this reading, hearts might be softened toward those who've suffered and who continue to suffer loss. That we might, with the heart of Jesus, love all people, respect all people. No matter their differences to ourselves.

If you've read an original version of *The Untold Stories*, you might have noticed that Nokose's death is depicted differently there. As I mentioned in that compilation's notes, I'd always intended to create a story that showed his final moments. It was supposed to happen in *Finding Pretty Wolf.* Alas, her story didn't allow that. This one did but required I change how he died. Thanks for allowing me the authorial liberty to do that.

With that, I'll close out this series and this season of my writing career. Next up, my venture into Bible studies and biblical fiction! Watch for them in late 2023.

Acknowledgements

Before I close out, I'd like to thank a few special people for their contributions to this story. My first thanks must always go to my Savior who gives me the inspiration and strength to write. Next, my hat comes off to Professor Cortez. Without her creative writing course, this story might never have come about. Special thanks also go out to two classmates, Melissa and Alyssa, for their input on the story's progression. Finally, my faithful beta readers have done it again. Jennifer, Rebekah, Laverne, and Therese came alongside me at the end and took *We Are Come to Die* to the finish line. Love and appreciation to you all!

And to you, my faithful reader friend, God bless you.

-- April

Glossary

Breechcloth: a long rectangular piece of animal hide or cloth that was brought up between the legs and under a belt at the waist. The ends hung like a flap over the belt in front and behind. Worn as outerwear by men and sometimes as underwear by women.

Che-lo-kee: extinct spelling of Cherokee.

Creek Confederacy: formed by survivors of the devastation wrought by 16th-century Spanish expeditions. The Muscogee were the strongest tribe at the time, and over the course of one hundred plus years, accepted refugee tribes under the umbrella of their protection. At its peak, it was so mighty George Washington treated the confederacy on a level of respect equal to that of France and Britain. The Creek War of 1813-14 began its decline.

Four-day Spirit Journey: the number of days it was believed to take for a soul to journey to the darkening land.

Lineage: a Creek's closest blood relatives, specifically those who lived together in the same family settlement. The Creek social system was organized as follows: individual, lineage, clan, town. The Creeks were a matrilineal society, meaning their blood (and clan) was traced through the women. Although a man was involved in his children's lives, he was not their blood relative nor was he ultimately responsible for their upbringing.

Maddo (mah-DOH): thank you (Muskogee language).

Medicine Bundle: small items wrapped in a package and worn by warriors for spiritual protection. Items varied from individual to individual but each held special significance to that warrior.

Micco (ME-koh), talwa (TAL-wuh): town chief. There were many levels of micco in both civil and military roles. This particular title was political.

Muscogees: an indigenous people who once dominated the Southeast. They occupied land from the Atlantic coast to central Alabama and were the founders of the Creek Confederacy. Also known as the Creeks.

Muskogee: language spoken by the Creeks and Seminoles.

Pawa (PAH-wuh): maternal uncle. A pawa oversaw the discipline and training of his sisters' sons. See elder brother. (Muskogee language.)

Red Sticks: 1. one of two social labels available to Creek men (Red Sticks/White Sticks). Red Sticks were known for courage, strength, alertness, physical skills.

They held leadership roles in warfare, security, and law enforcement. So called because of the red war club, the symbol of war. **2.** During the Creek War, the term "Red Stick" took on new meaning for the white settlers. For the duration of the war, a Red Stick was a Creek warrior who opposed the Americans; however, many warriors of the white persuasion shared their views and fought alongside them.

Sight, a: as far as one could see. Rough equivalent to our mile.

Sleeps: the marking of days or the passage of time. One sleep equals one day.

Sofkee: a thin gruel made of cornmeal or rice. Cooked with wood-ash lye and often eaten after being left to sour.

Sun Spirit: female; one of the four law-giving elements. Source of all light and life. Also known as Grandmother Sun.

The Floridas: the combination name given the two regions of Florida (West Florida and East Florida) which existed during the setting of this book. In 1813, both were owned by Spain. Also called Las Floridas.

Under World: the lowest of the Indian three-world cosmos. Existed below the earth and water. Epitomized chaos.

Upper World: the highest of the Indian three-world cosmos. Existed above the sky. Epitomized order.

Water Spirit: female; one of the four law-giving elements. Takes the form of rivers, lakes, rain, mist, streams, and the ocean.

White Sticks: 1. one of two social labels available to Creek men. White Sticks were known for reasonability, patience, mediation skills, scientific knowledge. Their roles included medicine maker, civil duties, diplomacy, ensuring of peace. **2.** During the Creek War, the term "White Stick" took on new meaning. For the duration of the war a White Stick was a Creek warrior who allied with the Americans; however, many warriors of the Red persuasion shared their views and fought alongside them.

www.ingramcontent.com/pod-product-compliance
Lightning Source LLC
Chambersburg PA
CBHW070519200726
48293CB00007B/2594